WOOF
GOES TO SCHOOL

by Danae Dobson
Illustrated by Dee deRosa

WORD PUBLISHING
Dallas · London · Sydney · Singapore

This book is dedicated to my mother, Shirley Dobson,
whom I dearly love. She has devoted her life
to the well-being of our family
and continues to demonstrate the qualities
of a godly wife and mother.
I will always appreciate her loving influence on my life.

Woof Goes to School

Copyright © 1989 by Danae Dobson for the text. Copyright © 1989 by Dee deRosa for the illustrations. All rights reserved. No portion of this book may be reproduced in any form without the written permission of the publishers, except for brief quotations in reviews.

Library of Congress Cataloging-in-Publication Data

Dobson, Danae.

  Woof goes to school.

  Summary: As Mark and Krissy work to find homes for six abandoned dogs, they are reminded that God loves even the unlovely.

  [1. Dogs — Fiction. 2. Animals — Treatment — Fiction. 3. Christian life — Fiction] I. DeRosa, Dee, ill. II. Title.

PZ7.D6614Wt 1989   [E]   89-22476

ISBN 0-8499-8348-7

Printed in the United States of America

9801239RA987654321

A MESSAGE FROM
Dr. James Dobson

Before you read about this dog named Woof perhaps you would like to know how these books came to be written. When my children, Danae and Ryan, were young, I often told them stories at bedtime. Many of those tales were about pet animals who were loved by people like those in our own family. Later, I created more stories while driving the children to school in our car pool. The kids began to fall in love with these pets, even though they existed only in our minds. I found out just how much they loved these animals when I made the mistake of telling them a story in which one of their favorite pets died. There were so many tears I had to bring him back to life!

These tales made a special impression on Danae. At the age of twelve, she decided to write her own book about her favorite animal, Woof, and see if Word Publishers would like to print it. She did, and they did, and in the process she became the youngest author in Word's history. Now, ten years later, Danae has written five more, totally new adventures with Woof and the Petersons. And she is still Word's youngest author!

Danae has discovered a talent God has given her, and it all started with our family spending time together, talking about a dog and the two children who loved him. We hope that not only will you enjoy Woof's adventures but that you and your family will enjoy the time spent reading them together. Perhaps you also will discover a talent God has given you.

It was the end of a long and enjoyable summer. Once again a new school year was starting, and all the children in the city of Gladstone would be returning to the classroom. Already the first golden, autumn leaves had begun to sprinkle the sidewalks along Maple Street, and with less sunshine the air had become a little cooler.

On the first morning, before it was time to leave, Mark and Krissy Peterson hurried around the house, putting on socks and shoes and gathering up book bags. Woof, their dog, sat in the background watching as they got ready. He understood the excitement because he had seen children go to school before. But he felt unhappy that Mark and Krissy would be leaving. Woof had had so much fun with the children since he came to live with them.

"Breakfast is ready!" Mrs. Peterson called from the kitchen.

Mark and Krissy hurried downstairs to the breakfast table with Woof right behind them.

"Boy, I hope I have Mrs. Thomas for a teacher this year," six-year-old Mark commented.

Mr. Peterson laughed. "I'm sure you'll do fine with whatever teacher you have."

After they had finished eating, Mark and Krissy gathered up their belongings and said good-bye to their mother and father. They both gave Woof a pat on the head as they headed for the driveway. Woof stood whimpering by the front door. He watched the children as they made their way across the street and around the corner, never taking his eyes off them for a minute! Finally it became too hard for him to stay put. Woof ran to catch up with his young friends.

When Mark and Krissy saw him coming, they scolded him for following them. "Woof, you can't come to school with us. Now go home!" Krissy said.

Woof stood with his crooked tail wagging and his tongue hanging out.

"Go on, boy. Go home!" Mark ordered, pointing toward their house.

Woof sadly turned and started back toward home, but as soon as Mark and Krissy began walking, he followed them again. This time they didn't see the dog behind them. Woof continued to trail his friends all the way to Mark's first grade classroom.

No one noticed the dog peeking around the doorway as the students took their seats. Then the teacher spoke. "Good morning, class. I am Mrs. Thomas," she said, standing at the chalkboard.

Suddenly Woof spotted Mark sitting in the front of the room and barked a loud greeting to his master. All the children turned at the same time to see a scraggly mutt with a crooked ear, wagging his tail back and forth excitedly. They burst out laughing as they pointed and waved at the confused dog.

Mark was surprised and embarrassed. "Oh, no!" he thought. "How did Woof get in here?"

Before he had a chance to react, a big kid in the back jumped out of his chair and made a lunge toward the dog. Woof became frightened and ran down the hallway.

"Catch that mutt!" someone shouted as he dashed by the office.
The principal and two teachers began chasing Woof through the building. The dog skidded around a corner and came to the end of the hall. Now he was trapped! What could he do? The principal and teachers quickly surrounded Woof, and one of them tied a rope around his neck. He was then

led into the school office and put in a corner. Woof knew he had done something wrong. He also knew he should have listened to Mark and Krissy when they told him to go home. Now he was in trouble, and there was no way out.

After an hour a white van from the city pound stopped in front of the school. Two men got out and went into the office. Seeing that Woof had no dog tag, they led him outside and into the back of the van. Woof did not know why he was being taken away from the school. Nor did he understand that the men were from the place where stray dogs and cats are kept. He did know he was frightened and alone. He also had a feeling the men were not taking him back to his home on Maple Street. And he was right.

Meanwhile Mark and Krissy had searched the school grounds looking for their lost dog. All during recess they looked for Woof, but he had simply disappeared. Finally they decided he had probably gone home. The children hadn't seen Woof being taken to the office and didn't know the men from the pound had come.

If only they had known Woof was in serious trouble! The big van pulled up in front of a small building, and Woof was taken from the back. He was then brought into a room and shoved inside a wire cage. The cage was dirty and uncomfortable, and the room smelled awful! Six other dogs were around him in cages like his. The dogs barked and howled miserably. Woof had never been to a pound before — even when he had been a stray before the Petersons adopted him. He hated this place and wanted more than anything to go home.

Woof anxiously looked around the room at the scrawny dogs in their cages. There was a big golden retriever, a bulldog and a chihuahua among the others. Right next to him lay an old, toothless hound. He was skinny and looked tired as he lay motionless on the floor of his cage. Although several flies buzzed around his nose, he didn't even try to fight them off. Only his eyes moved as he lay in the uncomfortable wire box.

Woof began to get more frightened as time went by. He wished he could have a good meal and be in his soft bed at home. And he wanted more than anything to see the Peterson family again. Would he ever find his way home? Would he ever run and play with Mark and Krissy again? Woof lay down sadly on the floor of his cage and rested his head on his feet. The other dogs continued to bark and whine, and the stale smell of the room was terrible.

After a long time an assistant at the pound came in with a large bucket. He went around to the cages and dumped some of the contents into each dish. Woof sniffed at the food, but he didn't want to eat it. He just wasn't hungry. For the first time in his life, Woof had lost his appetite. He could only think about how miserable he was and how much he missed his family.

Back at the Peterson house, Mark and Krissy had come home and found that Woof was not there. By six o'clock they were very worried. Something was definitely wrong. Mr. and Mrs. Peterson tried to be hopeful, but deep inside they were worried, too. Where could Woof be? He had never run away before.

By the time bedtime came around, the children were in tears.

"Let's pray for Woof, shall we?" Mother suggested.

Mark and Krissy knelt down by their beds and asked the Lord to protect their pet. They also prayed that the Lord would help them to find Woof wherever he was and to bring him home soon.

Everyone felt better after they had given the problem to Jesus. It made it easier to go to sleep that night, but they still missed their special friend.

The next morning while the children were getting ready for school, the telephone rang. Mrs. Peterson answered it. In a few moments, she happily called Mark and Krissy downstairs.

"That was a boy named Brian from the school," she said. "He saw Woof being taken away to the city pound yesterday."

"The pound!" Mark and Krissy shouted at the same time. They were so glad Woof had been found that they weren't as angry about the pound as they might have been.

"At least we know where Woof is," Mark said happily.

Mrs. Peterson called the school and told the secretary the children would be late. But before they left to pick up Woof, Mark and Krissy knelt down and thanked Jesus for answering their prayers. They were so glad Woof wasn't gone forever.

When they arrived at the pound, Mark and Krissy rushed past all the assistants in search of their beloved friend. They followed the sound of barking dogs into a back room.

"Woof!" Mark shouted, spotting him in one of the cages.

Woof pricked up his crooked ears and jumped to his feet. He began wagging his tail happily and barking. He was so glad to see the children he could hardly stay in one place! Mark and Krissy ran over to where he was and reached inside to pet him. In a few seconds Mother came in with an assistant to unlock the cage. As soon as Woof was released, he jumped all over the children, licking their faces and thrashing his tail back and forth. The children were just as happy to see him, too.

But no one seemed to notice the other dogs who had been watching the Peterson family and their pet. As the family prepared to leave, Woof turned and looked again at the toothless hound, who still lay in his miserable condition. The old dog gazed back at him with his tired, sad eyes. Then Woof looked across the room at all the other dogs. They had stopped barking and were watching him quietly. They all wished they had happy families to love them, too.

When Mark turned
and saw that Woof was
not following them, he became
puzzled. "Woof!" he called. "What's the matter?"

"I understand," Krissy said. "Woof feels sorry for the other dogs that don't have families to love them."

"It is a sad situation," Mother said. "I wish we could do something."

On the way to school the next morning, the two children talked about the homeless dogs. They knew their parents would never allow them to adopt all six. Besides, they already had Woof, and no dog could ever take his place. Nevertheless, the Peterson children were determined to help Woof's friends if they could. They just needed to think of a plan. Father suggested that they go around the neighborhood to find homes, but Mark had already tried that with Woof before they decided to adopt him. It didn't work.

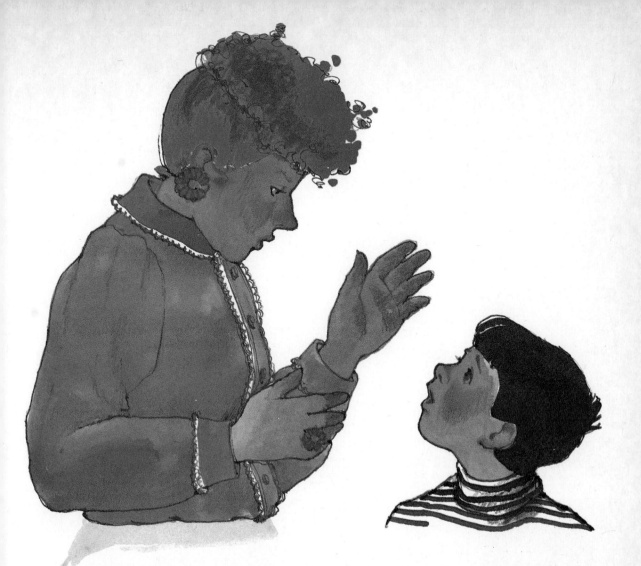

Still, the children continued to try to come up with a good solution. They asked friends and teachers around school if anyone knew of a way they could help, but no one seemed to have any ideas.

Finally Mark's teacher, Mrs. Thomas, came up with a suggestion. "Why don't you print some fliers and pass them around?" she asked. "That would be a great way to advertise, and it wouldn't cost very much."

"Hey, that's a great idea!" Mark said. "Maybe someone out there will give a home to those lost dogs."

When Mark told Krissy about Mrs. Thomas' idea, she agreed that it might work.

"Now we have to decide what we want the fliers to say," Mark said excitedly.

That afternoon the two children worked on the project at the kitchen table. When they were finished, this is what they had written:

<u>PLEASE</u> <u>HELP</u> save six homeless dogs at the city pound. These dogs are lonely and they need someone to love them. Here are the names we have given to the "Sad Six."

1. "Old Charlie": He's a little old, but very lovable hound dog.
2. "Freeway": a tiny Chihuahua that was picked up on the highway.
3. "Peppy": a gray terrier that runs and jumps all the time.
4. "Rusty": a golden retriever with a beautiful copper-colored fur coat.
5. "Trixie": a poodle who must have been in a circus act, because of all the tricks she can do.
6. "Rocky": a bulldog who could help protect your home.

<u>PLEASE CALL</u> Mark or Krissy Peterson if you could love and care for one of these dogs.

Phone: 782-4652   THANK YOU.

The next day at school, with Mrs. Thomas' help Mark made 200 copies of
the flier in the library and began to post them in the building. He put them
on bulletin boards, lockers and doorways. In between classes he handed
them out to students as they passed on their way to the playground. Luckily
his friend Barney Martin came by to help with the job. Together they had
given away most of the fliers by the end of the school day.

Mark decided to distribute the rest of them around the neighborhood. After
he had finished his homework, he got on his bicycle and rode up and down
the streets with Woof right beside him. When Mark came to a particular
house, he would give Woof a flier, and the dog would carry it to the doorway
and set it down. After an hour they had distributed the last of the copies.

When Mark and Woof returned to their house, Krissy met them at the door. "The phone has been ringing and ringing," she said happily. "I've had twelve calls from people who are interested in the dogs."

"That's great!" Mark said. "Maybe those poor animals will have homes and people to love just like Woof."

The rest of the night was spent returning phone calls from children and teachers who had seen the fliers posted at school. By bedtime the Petersons had received forty-two calls.

"Imagine that," Mother sighed. "Forty-two calls for only six dogs."

Mark did not respond as he cast his eyes down.

"What's the matter?" Father asked, sensing that something was wrong.

"The phone calls have only been for five dogs — not six. No one wants Old Charlie," Mark said sadly. "I just couldn't stand to leave him alone in that wire cage. He looks so pitiful."

Father seemed to be lost in thought as he sat in his big chair. Finally, after a couple of minutes, he spoke. "There is nothing to feel guilty about, son," he said softly. "You have provided five homeless animals with a place to live. You should feel proud of what you have done."

Mark nodded his head. "I guess you're right. Maybe someone will change his mind about Old Charlie."

"I wouldn't count on that," Father said. "Nobody is going to want an old, useless dog like that. He would only be a burden."

Deep inside Mark knew his father was right. There was little chance anyone would want to adopt such an animal. All Mark could do was wait and hope that someone would call.

The next morning the sun shone brightly through the window on a warm Saturday. Mark and Krissy were up early because today they would be picking up the dogs at the pound and delivering them to the families that wanted them. Mark's friend Barney Martin had called and said his father would drive his pick-up truck out to get the dogs. Everything had worked out perfectly — well, almost everything.

At 9:30, Mr. Martin and Barney arrived at the Petersons' home. The children put Woof in the back of the truck, and they crawled into the front seat. It was a little bit crowded, but they managed to squeeze in. In just a little while, the truck pulled into the parking lot of the city pound.

"Excuse me," Mark said, walking through the double doors at the entrance.

A middle-aged woman at a desk looked up. "Yes?" she said. "Can I help you?"

"My name is Mark Peterson, and I've come to pick up five of the dogs."

The woman looked a little surprised. By this time Krissy and the Martins had caught up with Mark. Woof circled around the room, sniffing the air. He remembered being there just a few days before. It was not a good memory for him.

The woman cleared her throat. "Right this way," she directed.

Mr. Martin waited while the children and Woof followed her down the hallway and into the bad-smelling room. The dogs had been barking and howling, but they stopped when they saw the children. How happy they were when the woman unlocked all their cages! In just a few seconds, five excited dogs were barking and running all around the room. The children laughed at the sight of them. But in a few moments, their laughter stopped.

Over in the corner sat Woof, next to the cage where
Old Charlie lay. Woof whined and gently pushed the latch
that held the dog captive, but he could not open it. The old dog
stood up on his wobbly legs and looked helplessly at the children.

Krissy was almost certain she saw a tear in his eyes. "I can't stand to
look," she said.

"Me either," Mark agreed. "Come on, let's go. There's nothing we can do."
With that, the three children and all the dogs headed toward the truck. Woof
took one last look at his tired, old friend and slowly turned and left the room.

Five dogs barked happily all the way home in the back of the truck — but not Woof, who was still sad about the old hound dog. Woof understood what it was like to feel unwanted and unloved. Before he was adopted by the Peterson family, he had traveled the streets alone, with no one to love. He wished he could do something for the poor dog at the pound, but he knew it was beyond his control.

One by one the children delivered the dogs to the families that wanted them. Krissy had an address sheet and told Mr. Martin where to drive. Before long, each member of the "sad five" had a home. Mark and Krissy said good-bye to Barney and thanked Mr. Martin for his help. They felt happy as they walked home, but they had not forgotten about the sixth dog — worn-out, pitiful Old Charlie.

Just then, in the distance, the children noticed an elderly man walking toward them slowly with the help of a cane. He staggered along the street and met them just as they reached the driveway of their house. He was holding one of the fliers Mark had printed.

"Would you happen to be the Peterson children?" he asked, his eyes searching their faces.

"Yes," Mark answered.

The old man smiled. "My name is Mr. Robinson, and I live down on the corner of Maple Street. I was taking a walk this afternoon and thought I would stop by and ask you about the advertisement for the dogs."

"I'm sorry, Mister, but all the dogs have been given away," Mark said.

"There's only one left, and he's an old hound dog. I don't know if you'd be interested in him," said Krissy hopefully.

"Why, that's just the kind of dog I am interested in," Mr. Robinson replied. "You see, I'm old, too. I've lived a good life, but I just don't have very much energy anymore. I think an old hound and I would get along just fine. I could use a needy friend."

Mark and Krissy grabbed each other and shouted.

"That's great!" Mark exclaimed. "Old Charlie is still at the pound. If you'd like, I'm sure my parents would give you a ride down there."

"Thank you," Mr. Robinson said. "I'm far too old to drive a car anymore. But if someone could give me a ride, I would like to take a look at the dog."

After Mr. Robinson had left, Mark and Krissy ran into the house to tell their parents the good news. Their mother and father were delighted and agreed to drive Mr. Robinson to the pound that afternoon.

"Wouldn't it be something if Mr. Robinson would want to keep Old Charlie?" Krissy said. Mark and Krissy hugged each other and jumped up and down. Woof didn't understand why everyone was so happy, but he knew something good was happening.

Later that afternoon the Peterson family and Mr. Robinson pulled into the parking lot of the pound. Even Woof went along for the ride.

They all followed Mr. Robinson into the room where Old Charlie lay. The Petersons and Woof stood at the door and watched as the elderly man slowly made his way over to the cage. He gently reached inside to stroke Old Charlie on the head. There seemed to be an instant bond of love between the man and the dog as their eyes met for the first time. Old Charlie licked Mr. Robinson's hand with his warm, pink tongue. After a few moments Mr. Robinson looked up. "Unlock the cage," he said to the assistant. "I'll take him."

Mark and Krissy could hardly keep from shouting as Old Charlie was released from his miserable condition. Even Woof stood with his tail banging against the wall.

Mr. Robinson turned toward the family and smiled. "This old hound will make a perfect friend for me. Given our age, we'll probably get to heaven about the same time."

The Peterson family watched as Mr. Robinson and Old Charlie limped out of the door and down the hall together. They were glad they had found one another.

As the Petersons followed behind, Mark wiped a tear from his eye. "Do you know what?" he asked. "I believe the Lord even cares about an old dog like Charlie, don't you?"

"Yes," Krissy answered. "And if he cares that much about a dog that nobody wanted, just think how much He must love you and me! He loved us so much that he sent his only Son to die for us. And that is real love."